Lewis Gilbert Wilson

Glimpses of a Better Life in the Journey of Experience

Lewis Gilbert Wilson

Glimpses of a Better Life in the Journey of Experience

ISBN/EAN: 9783744799577

Printed in Europe, USA, Canada, Australia, Japan

Cover: Foto ©Andreas Hilbeck / pixelio.de

More available books at **www.hansebooks.com**

GLIMPSES

OF

A BETTER LIFE

IN

The Journey of Experience

BY

LEWIS GILBERT WILSON

CAMBRIDGE

JOHN WILSON AND SON

University Press

1892

TO

The Memory of Our Little Boy,

Who, having entered in by the gates into the city, has left us great assurances,

THIS BOOK IS DEDICATED.

CONTENTS.

OUR life itself, in its countless mazes, in the bitter and sweet of its experience, in its depths of emotion and lifts of thought; the imagination, nourished and enriched by all we have felt and thought and seen and known; the soul, with such wealth of capacity and mastery of passion as it may have won, — this must, after all, make for every man the mirror, which at every point reflects some different aspect of the universe, and at every turn does something to brighten or deepen the picture that images to us the Universal Life. To a mind religiously trained that picture is what we call "the thought of God."

J. H. ALLEN (*Positive Religion*).

GLIMPSES OF A BETTER LIFE.

———•———

CHAPTER I.

THE VASTER LIFE.

I.

THE one subject of paramount interest to the human soul is Life. Infancy, adolescence, maturity, and the myriad mysteries therein involved, are always new to the individual student. As every one of the earth's countless inhabitants is the heir of the whole of Time, so the whole of life is the natural dower of each sentient creature. He may fail to grasp it, he may grasp and then squander or bury it; but it is his nevertheless, by natural right. As the atmosphere to man's lungs, so is life to his soul,—with this difference however, that whereas the atmosphere envelops this particular globe on which we dwell, life is the element of, and is coextensive with, the universe. Little systems have been marked out by the intellect which included the phenomena and essence of this sphere only; but a new conception — of a vast federation of peopled planets — is just finding its way into the day-dreams of humanity.

> " There is no end to God's
> Domain of suns, and systems ruled by suns, —
> No end and no beginning through all space ;
> But everlasting, mystic, wonderful,
> The song of us sounds ever round the throne
> Of Him who reigns supreme, the Life of all."

And yet this expansion of the field of thought increases rather than diminishes the enigmas of pain and joy and triumph. The momentous questions which arise in the presence of birth, youth, age, and death are in no final sense answered in the widened ranges of man's intellectual advancement. Still, as in the earliest days, he is caught in the colossal flash-light, and knows not the character of the darkness which follows, or seems to follow. One truth alone evermore appeals to him for acceptance, — that he is a part of a vaster scheme of things than he had ever previously imagined. Wider and higher and deeper the realm extends on every side, with every new discovery man makes ; and, therefore, more and more valid becomes to his mental life that true faith which is " the conviction of things not seen." Whatever then can in any way impart or increase that faith within his restless, inquiring, longing spirit should find its way to the world.

II.

The conception of Eden is native to the individual. It is the result of his backward gaze from the trials, pitfalls, disappointments, and sins of after-life to the innocent charms of childhood and youth. Now that they have passed away, the early days rise up to fill the human heart with the sweet anguish of de-

parted joys. All there is, or ever was, or
ever could be, in the legends of Eden is
suggested here, —

> "Ye banks and braes o' bonny Doon,
>   How can ye bloom sae fresh and fair;
>   How can ye chant, ye little birds,
>   And I sae weary, fu' o' care?
>   Thou 'lt break my heart, thou warbling bird,
>   That wantons through the flowering thorn;
>   Thou minds me o' departed joys,
>   *Departed — never to return!*"

Such a sense of a bright and beautiful past,
hidden now behind clouds of varied experience, could alone have been the inspiration of
Faust, — the poem of poems, —

> "Give me, oh, give me back the days
> When I — I too — was young,
> And felt, as they now feel, each coming hour
> New consciousness of power.
> Oh, happy, happy time, above all praise!
> Then thoughts on thoughts and crowding fancies sprung,
> And found a language in unbidden lays,
> Unintermitted streams from fountains ever flowing.
>   Then, as I wandered free,
>   In every field for me

Its thousand flowers were blowing !
A veil through which I did not see,
A thin veil o'er the world was thrown
In every bud a mystery ;
Magic in everything unknown.
The fields, the grove, the air was haunted,
And all that age has disenchanted.
Yes ! give me, give me back the days of youth,
Poor, yet how rich ! — my glad inheritance
The inexhaustible love of truth,
While life's realities were all romance —
Give me, oh, give youth's passions unconfined,
The rush of joy that felt almost like pain,
Its hate, its love, its own tumultuous mind ;
Give me my youth again ! "

Wherever the memory of the adult revives and ponders over the joys and anticipations of youth, this cry for the early days breaks forth. Opportunities neglected, hopes unrealized, prayers unanswered, barren attainments, and the consciousness of deadened sensibilities awaken in the human heart, at that moment when it enters upon the grave responsibilities and struggles of experience, a longing for the return of years which have forever passed away. And then, too, one begins to decipher revelations before unknown. The generation which treads upon the heels of the one to which he belongs seems all alive with prophetic voices, or over-written, like some crowded palimpsest, with the mysterious characters which evermore instruct mankind concerning what it ought to be and is not. A thousand influences tend toward regret, a thousand admonish to a higher and nobler career; and it is only after long meditation, after superlative endeavor, after self-renunciation and the new birth of the spirit into the realm of genuine faith, that the troubled soul finds peace. That journey is long and perilous. It begins its varied course where infancy teaches the character of the first Eden. Infancy is prophetic, and points over the heads of the fathers to the kingdom of God, instructing the fathers, and affording them, in its guileless purity, the incentive to labor, to pray, and to wait if so be they may obey the commands of its sinless evangels.

CHAPTER II.

I.

BLESSED are the child-faces of the world! In those faces behold we the justification for rejoicing in the truth, bearing all things, believing all things, hoping all things, and enduring all things. They hold us to the essential principles of the swift world, and without them we should slip into the abyss of our own undoing.

Whether welcome or unwelcome (and where unwelcome Nature blushes) they enter here with a cry of triumph, as of conquerors into a defeated realm. And with what perfect dignity they ascend their thrones! They are the only rulers by divine right. They come with their own standards, with their own methods. With as much power of unconsciousness as Napoleon possessed of self-consciousness, they set at nought all the precedents of history. You cannot bribe them. Silver and gold are not precious metals in their sight. Will not tin and brass do as well? And where the " wise and prudent" might gain favor by means of title and lineage, they come to grace with knighthood the beggar and the serf. They behold features beneath masks, and hear the spirit and learn of what stuff it is, despite studied elocution. Of all the world they can return a kiss for a blow. They are " of the kingdom."

And is it not apparent that all other claims of royalty are based on transient foundations? All other sovereigns are made by men, but these by the Eternal. All others are artificial, but these are natural. The earth whirls, that on it babes may come and reign. To this end the globe exists. Is not this the teaching of Evolution, — that civilization receives its credentials from the cradle and is made possible by the extension of the period of infancy ? So long as in the mollusk birth meant maturity, there was and could be no rapid upward trend. But when mothers began to weep for their offspring, the Edens of life were watered, and the desert began to blossom as the rose. Art, industry, schools, colleges, and churches exist at the command of infancy.

Nature seeks birth. What follows is of less moment. Birth is the event of the universe. To remain here after birth is a matter of indifference with Nature, for there are more forces to destroy than to preserve the physical creature. The great majority of all who are born into this world simply pass by us, like swift angels, or bright flashes of light, to the end which justifies birth. The minority remain to make other births possible, and to linger through joy, pain, bereavement, anxiety, and peace, until the second generation is well equipped for the same labors. Thus are the relays of life brought forth in this mys-

terious journey of the earth from chaos to the
Life of all. But the child-faces, what of
them?

II.

Therein is no faintest trace of sin. Such
faces ought ever to be about us in this first
life. "Of such is the kingdom." In those
faces there are worlds of expression, but no
expression of the "world." Pure, ingenuous,
frank, and trustful, the great, saving elements of life beam there, — shine forth from
their bright eyes and speak from their lips un-
defiled. They are our perpetual reminders of
faith and virtue. Parchments are they from
which the divine message has not been erased.
Oh, if it could be allowed to remain, or made
to become ever more clear and full and constant! How soon self-consciousness spreads
its foolish, drivelling mask over features made
in heaven! How soon vanity, and then
through vanity, lust and the execrable records
of guilt and folly place their characters where

only the shining beatitudes were meant to be written! And how soon the pitiful proof-marks of disappointment and mental or moral conflict get imprinted on our facile human brows!

The frailest babe has much to teach us if we sit at its feet. It may not speak to us, but its face has many a gleam of heavenly wisdom, — just faint traces of a large and beneficent and divine revelation of the soul. Thus it is made to appear that —

> "Our birth is but a sleep and a forgetting :
>   The soul that rises with us, our life's star,
>   Hath had elsewhere its setting,
>   And cometh from afar :
>   Not in entire forgetfulness,
>   Not in utter nakedness,
>   But trailing clouds of glory do we come
>   From God, who is our home.
>   Heaven lies about us in our infancy ! "

Because they bring inarticulate revelations of a loftier realm than this, we have this loyalty of our nature to the tyranny of infancy.

III.

Few are they who do not possess this loyalty. It levels all distinctions. If it is true of the hovel, it is likewise true of the palace. To win smiles and favors from such royalty, the proudest will grovel. Orphan asylums are the first charities of all progressive peoples; for those who have none must needs care for others' children, either directly or indirectly, at the bidding of that helplessness which is more potent than despotism. With its coming to the rudest dwelling come refinements, which otherwise were impossible. The babe says, " Let there be health, gentility, art, religion," and they are. The roughest man becomes a gentleman or a bowing, smiling courtier in the presence of his new babe. And many an atheist, upon whom the priesthood and the Church had wrought in vain, has seen God and confessed immortality in the nursery of his own children. The worst of drunkards must have lucid moments wherein to pray that his little ones may never come to his misery; and the thief, that they may be able to resist temptation. In the presence of his own daughter what father worthy the name would not be chaste and true!

With their own patient hands parents make the beds, prepare the food, and with a love not lightly to be spoken of watch over their offspring. And yet they have felt that their children were their protectors. Safer with than without them! Wherein their power may be man may not say, but the children save us when the test comes. If the sands rise about our feet, will not God and Christ and all the saints save us for the baby's sake?

Calvin had no children, else he had had less logic; for the wisdom of babes and sucklings outstrips, and ever will outstrip, that of the wise and understanding. Be their system never so perfect to man's discursive sense, if it leaves out of account any of the mysterious forces that bind fathers, mothers, and babes, it must fall. Men could ever populate hell with other people's children, but never seriously with their own. Thus it is that childhood reverses and subdues the decrees of the wise, setting at nought the judgments of men, and revealing, in spite of our self-imposed blindness, glimpses of a better life. And what of childlikeness?

IV.

All true insight urges man to preserve it as the precious jewel of life, — to cherish, reverence, and transmit it as the legacy of the past, and the promise of a future heaven. It is the chief gift, next to life itself, of the Father's hand. To wear it is to brighten, cheer, emancipate, and exalt the world! Where is sadness and shame except where that jewel is injured or lost? Where is kingly strength except where it is retained, in all its pristine beauty? Is it not the talisman of virtue? Where it disappears there

Art seeks to make up for what is lost.   Then
comes the imitation, where the original was
meant to be, — the ghastly makeshift!   No
decorations, no gems, no beautiful fabric;
no grace or movement of head or hand, no
posture nor attitude of feature, can put back
into the human eye what is *lost* with the loss
of innocence.   All garniture fails here; the
schools fail here; society miserably fails
here.   Here all the charms of art only make
more pitiful the absence of the charms of
nature.   If only men and women could preserve unimpaired what trouble and care and
temptation and sin so often rob them of,
they might exclaim, "I am a king; to this
end have I been born, and to this end am I
come into the world, that I should bear witness unto the truth:" and if there were not
on all our faces the scars of moral burning
— traces of defeated manhood and womanhood — even demons would see and hear.
Blessed children!

" We need love's tender lessons, taught
    As only weakness can;
God hath his small interpreters,
    The child must teach the man.

   .   .   .   .   .

The haughty eye shall seek in vain
    What innocence beholds ;
No cunning finds the key of heaven,
    No strength its gates unfolds.

Alone to guilelessness and love
    That gate shall open fall ;
The mind of pride is *nothingness,*
    The childlike heart is all."

We support them in the world, prepare
them to meet and endure the world, protect
them for a time from the world; but they
teach and prepare us for the kingdom of God!

But when childhood and innocence have
fallen from us like the leaves of a summer
past, what then ? Are there still some
glimpses of a better life ?

CHAPTER III.

I.

NOTHING in the world can lend terror to the soul which sees through the shadows the divine realities. We cannot compromise with law, but we may get greater peace by observing and obeying law. The Past is forever guarded by a flaming sword, which turns every way to prevent our entrance again into its innocence and joy. And it is well, therefore, that we learn, at the earliest possible hour of life, that if fleet Time and reckless Fate drive us from one Eden, it is that we may, by grasping the better conditions of life as we are borne in its current, find even a nobler Paradise. Our first birth is into a world of innocence, of helpless love; of a nameless enjoyment of birds and flowers

and bright streams, and forests and fruits.
That Eden passes away. Let a simple reminiscence stand for the day and hour when
childhood ceased, and the struggle up the
hard highway of mortality began.

II.

Near the dear old home there arose a long
line of peaceful, happy hills. They bounded
the horizon at the north and northeast. With
green foliage were they covered in the spring
and early summer; with dreamy haze in late
summer and early autumn; with hues from
scarlet to brightest yellow in autumn; in
pure, cold white in winter. On their sides
the cattle fed over patches of pasture-land,
and here and there great bowlders lay always
like huge, sleeping elephants. To my childhood's fancy those hills were mysterious, —
very, very mysterious! I knew not what
might be beyond them. Perhaps the world
came to an end there, where the sky came
down like a curtain. The world was as new

to me then as to the ancients. The day was in October. Leaves had begun to grow too beautiful to describe. The thistle was sending forth its children into the bright sky, upborne in parachutes that could be trusted, beyond all kith and kin, never to return again. Already the cheerful finches had sung their flocking note, and into the distant clouds the smoke-wreaths of many a quiet hamlet were gathered quietly and were at rest. My brother and I were allowed to go that day on an exploring expedition to those hills that seemed so far away. Oh, what a daring undertaking it was! How suddenly I seemed to grow toward manhood when I really found that I was going so far away to visit the long, bright, patient, mysterious hills! A visit to the world's end would not awaken in me now such brave exhilaration. I had read about Robinson Crusoe, about Cortez, about adventurers on our western plains; but nothing could have increased the sense of adventure which attended the thought of this

wondrous enterprise. Well do I remember
looking back, after reaching the first knoll,
to see if the old house looked smaller! How
well I can now see the column of blue smoke
as it rose straight up from the great chimney!
To us boys every field was a prairie, every
stream a great river, every thicket a "forest
primeval," every wild apple-tree the natural
fruit of the virgin earth, before unknown to
the eye or palate of mortal man. We saw
hawks describing their great circles against
the blue zenith; and — as strange and pic-
turesque to us as to the followers of Colum-
bus were the bright flamingoes — were several
long-necked "squawking" herons. At last
we reached the hills. How marvellous the
ascent! From time to time we would look
back and name the distant farmhouses. We
could see two villages which — white clusters
of peaceful cottages that they were — seemed
like so many great cities. And when we
had nearly reached the summit, the spires of
far-off Hopkinton rose to view, — a sight

which thrilled us then as would now the
domes and minarets of Constantinople.
Climbing a tall tree which rose above the
others that crowned the summit, with as
much joy and sense of triumph as Balboa
must have felt when he looked out upon the
Pacific Ocean, we gazed upon the before unknown world beyond. There, behold! were
long rivers, smoke-laden cities, forests wild
and forbidding, shining lakes, and distant,
cloud-like mountains.

And then we came home, — to the meek,
humble, commonplace old home of mother
and father. It was nightfall, and we were
tired and hungry and sleepy, as only boys
can be after such a day as that. It was a
great day because it had changed the world.
Life was never the same to me again. My
horizon was extended, but oh, at what cost!
This earth became larger, but only at the
sacrifice of that near, sweet, brooding Eden
of the old roof-tree. A secret sense of having advanced, an unquenchable flame of ad-

venture, — which, in one way and another, would never cease to burn, — had been kindled. Hereafter I knew that no parental door-yard could contain and limit me! Whatever other years might reveal, the decree had gone forth to the uttermost bounds of that country which we call the Soul, and restlessness and dim apprehensions of struggle had supplanted forever the peace and trust of infancy.

III.

To pass on from that hour to the hour of the birth of the spirit, after the fierce travailings of experience, is as a journey through a pitiless and friendless wilderness. It is a journey through the uncertainty of Fate, the torments of doubt, through wastes of soul-sickening disappointment. But the end will, I trust, find us restored to the Life of all, wherein there is joy forevermore. Wild, dark, foreboding, and cruel is the wilderness just outside the first bright Eden of childhood and youth, but after that is the new birth, — the birth 'from above.

> " It is a new birth,
> A ray of immortality,"

it is when we behold, behind the shadows, the imperishable realities.

CHAPTER IV.

HOW SHALL I LIVE?

I.

MAN alone, of all God's creatures, lives consciously between a Past and a Future. Herein we differ, so far as we know, from the brutes. To them there appears little or no Past or Future. They seem to realize, and that only dimly, the Present. But man never stands still in Time. While it is true that all we have is the Present, yet it is likewise true that man has not and never had a Present; for when we have created even the faintest intellectual image of it, it has passed away.

" Yesterday the sullen year
   Saw the snowy whirlwind fly;
Mute was the music of the air,
   The herd stood drooping by :

Their raptures now that wildly flow,
No yesterday nor morrow know.
'T is man alone that joy descries
With forward or reverted eyes."

And now, after the brief moment of innocence is passed, what question presses upon
the mind of all? It is this: How shall I
live, and to what end? What shall be the
main purpose of my life? Shall I devote
this life to success? Shall I seek pleasure,
or even happiness, for its own sake? Shall
I struggle for eminence, or relax into com-
placence and peaceful indolence? Such is
the question which at life's crucial hour
awaits an answer, and will not be put off.
It is at the hour when youth emerges into
manhood or womanhood. And behold what
visions then appear! Great heights are beheld in dim outline, deep gulfs are appre-
hended. And then, too, our better angels
are heard near at hand, and we understand
them and resolve to follow them faithfully.
But unfortunately we soon get involved in

3

the shadows and forget the realities. We are thrown off our guard by untoward circumstance. The years pass swiftly away. As they come and go our duties and anxieties increase. Fainter and fainter become the ideals of youth. The noise of commerce, the roarings of trade, the jealousies of cliques and parties; the eager and selfish graspings after distinction and places of fame; the petty irritations that arise in the smallest circles; the unforeseen disappointments that somehow come forth where we had least expected them; the heartless events that crush us and become calamities because we had not prepared to meet them; dislodgements from positions of comfort and ease, — all these children of Experience throng upon us, and it wellnigh requires the gift of perennial youth — which no man hath — to rise above them and find joyance and justice in human life.

II.

Oh, how wild and reckless is this cruel Manipulator of human life ! He tosses us about without mercy. Man says, " Now I will do this and this ; I will build mansions this year ; I will read books, I will make journeys, I will have pleasure." He lays plans, and takes comfort in the thought of success. It seems worth all time and strength, all education and aspiration, to be " successful," — to make money, to ride in carriages, to travel, to move in society, to have seen sights. So great is the inundation of such interests as these that men forget to ask again and again, " How shall we live ? " And fortunate it is for those who ever come to see, even in mortifying humility, with what triumphant skill the demon of Time cunningly leads them on from one foolish purpose to another foolish purpose until foolish Habit gains ascendency over their will. In this labyrinth of chance and convulsive struggle life becomes but a senseless game, — a ruthless game, where everybody thinks that everybody is seeking to befool everybody, — a long and tedious masquerade! Is it not pitiful beyond the telling when men and women find themselves playing at a *game* of life, with their false faces, their conventional hypocrisies, their smirkings and mincings and shameless glossings of positive vices?

CHAPTER V.

I.

OH, remember then, if flames pour not down over your already blinded eyes, the moment when you stood at the parting of the way, and asked, "How shall I live?" You stood there! No life, however buoyant, however dazzled in the flame of pleasure, however pressed by circumstance, but has asked, or will ask that question. It was the moment when "deep called unto deep;" when the unsounded flood of the everlasting Divinity came furiously pouring over the trembling soul, to lift it, or submerge it. Above were the Eternities with their stars of hope smiling upon human aspiration, — beckoning with their fingers of light, to come ever toward them. All around were the verities and the mighty realities of the life that is, appealing to the eternal qualities of human nature. There Faith called for allegiance, there Duty demanded that her voice be heard. Nature sang of the imperishable truths of which she is but the symbol. If we could only call those moments back again! If they would come to us and bid us enter life anew! If we only could grasp them, and feel again the fresh, the nameless delight of youth and love and innocence, which caused all things to seem real and true and good! Call out, O baffled, crushed, mistaken, sin-sick spirit, call out for the early days! Bid Time turn back the sun and reverse the years, that you may awake and find this thoroughfare of life nought but a teeming and seething apparition, and all that seems a dreadful mockery the work of a fevered, laboring brain!

II.

This calling back of our burdened hearts for the early days, and these memories of

Paradise, are the never-ceasing birth-pangs
of the immortal part of us. Man cannot
cause the Sun to stand still upon Gibeon,
nor the Moon in the valley of Aijalon. He
cannot bring back the Past. Henceforth
there must be darkness, the unbroken sod,
the wild beast, the hunger and the cold.
But all this because man is able to meet it!
When he learns that he transcends all circumstance, man passes beyond defeat. The
time comes when the craving to solve the
enigmas of life sufficiently to gain the surpassing peace, is irresistible. He then goes
forward, and the first great difficulty of the
wilderness is transcended. He then knows
that, whatever the intervening struggles, he
will arrive, —

> " I go to prove my soul !
> I see my way as birds their trackless way.
> I shall arrive ! What time, what circuit first,
> I ask not : but unless God send his hail,
> Or blinding fire-balls, sleet, or stifling snow,
> In some good time, his good time, I shall arrive.
> He guides me and the bird. In his good time !"

And it is when this thought settles over his soul like a sweet balm, that other thoughts find their way into his reflections, of comfort and reconciliation.   He knows he cannot turn back.   Having entered the flood, he must now go on or drown.   But he cannot drown; so he knows that, engulfed in the single divine alternative, he is to go forward and arrive.   And then he begins to become a new creature.   Then, as in the worm the butterfly, so in his body terrestrial begin to form the rudiments of the body celestial; or, as in the far-off mass of floating protoplasm there were the dim prophecies of all organic life, so within his soul gather the faint centres of angelic being.   Then come thoughts of his greatness and his great destiny; then come other glimpses of a better life.

CHAPTER VI.

THE LONELINESS OF PROGRESS.

I.

ALL true progress is made in loneliness. The world-prophets in their hours of greatest agony and in the eve of their greatest triumphs have ever had occasion to say, even of their nearest and dearest companions, "What, canst thou not watch with me one hour?" No; not one hour! We have friends in our prosperity, friends in our sorrow, friends in our sickness, friends in our death; but friends to watch with us in the Gethsemane of the soul no man ever had. It is then we may talk with God, and only with God. The world may then be bright enough without, but it is lonely and dark within. None can know you then save yourself and God. And even then you cannot know yourself as God knows you.

It is the hour of moral triumph over re-
proach, over passion, over persecution, over
ignorance, and over the dead past. The
world cries, "See! one possessed of demons! let us stone him. 'He, being a man,
maketh himself a God.'" But that higher
Voice whispers, "Woe unto you when all
men shall speak well of you!" Our own
divinities must always rebuke us whenever
we level down our higher conceptions of duty
and truth to the realized standards of our
time and place. They rebuke us because
therein is the defeat of all progress. To arrive at Life, our individual lives must expand
to higher virtues. In us all there is the reflection of Nature's sternest moods. In spite
of itself the world shall be lifted. And if
at times it seems as if one man must bear
the awful burden, so it must be lifted.
Then are we all the world's redeemers, for
whosoever transcends one sin, transcends it
for all men. Every moral triumph of the
individual is a triumph for the world; else —

" The pillared firmament is rottenness
And earth's base built on stubble."

Thus it is we prove the soul, — prove it to
be more of God and heaven than of man and
the world. Cast out of the first Eden, we
walk on burning rays of light to the second
Eden. And the voices, and the child-faces,
and the happy memories of the past, and the
revelations that our eyes just begin to behold,
— all combine to give us courage and zeal.
Then are we no longer beggars knocking at
the gates for bread we have not earned. And,
sooner or later, the world itself sheds tears
of gratitude when it learns of one who was
steadfast when men reproached him; that one
meant them nought but good when the mul-
titudes jeered and hissed and stoned him;
that between him and his God there was no
cloud of unfaith; and that through good and
evil report, through lies, slander, and cow-
ardly insinuation, the compass of his being
was ever true to its lodestar. Waves of
deadly hate, of jealousy that is never weary

in wrong-doing, of cunning conspiracy and stupid scorn, may beat against the citadel of true manhood, lit by the grace of God; but sooner or later, the tide sleeps, and there is a great calm of gratitude over all the world.

II.

Surely, this is a fit truth to be cut in marble! In splendid and thrilling cadence, in distant moanings, murmurings, rollings, and thunderings like that of the sea, the great organ of St. Patrick's Cathedral throbs and swells. And as you enter, the glorious statue of John McNeil Boyd, who in 1861 was lost off the rocks at Kingston in attempting to rescue the crew of the "Neptune," stands before you. A coil of rope is in his right hand, in the act of throwing; his strong, broad shoulders thrown back; his head, erect and luminous, with flowing locks; his lips firm, and eyes intense, — it is a monument all instinct with the spirit of self-sacrificing heroism. In that splendid presence you read this inscription, —

"Safe from the rocks whence swept thy manly form,
The tide's white rush, the stepping of the storm,
Borne with a public pomp, by just decree,
Heroic sailor! from that fatal sea,
A city vows this marble unto thee.
And here, in this calm place, where never din
Of earth's great water-floods shall enter in;
Where to our human hearts two thoughts are given, —
One, Christ's self-sacrifice, the other heaven, —
Here it is meet for grief and love to grave
The Christ-taught bravery that died to save
The life not lost, but found beneath the wave."

The larger and better heroes of the world are ever like him, — hurling the line of self-sacrifice into the teeth of the storm. It is thus that their lives are not lost, " but found beneath the waves." Sooner or later the tide sleeps, and there is a great calm of gratitude over all the world.

III.

Our natures are really as mysterious and many-sided as the bright natural world about us. We have our definite ends in view. We may struggle through every sort of misrepresentation and injustice that we may carry out the behest of conscience; but woe to him who stops in that endeavor to explain his methods and give a foolish and curious multitude reasons for this or that! One might as well attempt to explain why any particular drop of water happens to fall on any particular blade of grass. The conditions are infinite. Does not such a task involve the lives and opinions of past generations? One has simply to seek strength in the consciousness of eternal rectitude. That consciousness no man ever found insufficient, but it impels to heroism; indeed, it impels to that which is the very essence of heroism, namely, — *love* of the heroic. That was the element which raised the soul of the lonely Thoreau above the need of human companionship; for his pen gathered fire when he had charged himself with the inspiration of the storm. His face must needs be cold and wet with the fierce sleet;

about the little hut his winds must blow, and the surface of the lake must be lashed into foaming whitecaps. It was when the earth shook and the hills screamed in echoing answer to the bellowing clouds that his brain teemed with living thought and transformed his skull into a temple of the gods. To man sensitized at the battery of all power and truth, man electrified by contact with the Life of all, there comes that which responds to all power, — even to that which is manifested in symbols of antagonism and devastation, rousing him to divine effort, and compelling him to sublime achievement. It is the heroism of the spirit which hastens and perfects our journey along Time's rugged and lonely pathway, and multiplies for us the blessed glimpses of a better life.

CHAPTER VII.

THE GUARDIANSHIP OF GOD.

I.

AND yet with what trembling and trepidation one comes to that consciousness of God which makes him a hero of the soul! At that very moment when he may begin to grasp the thought of his transcendency, he feels his utter insufficiency and weakness. "A little lower than God, and crowned with glory and honor," and fighting his way with consummate courage and skill in the very vortex of conflicting forces; and then, alas! the thought of his insignificance — "What is man that Thou art mindful of him, and the son of man that Thou visitest him?" Thus it is we move through the mind's wilderness in zigzag lines of confidence and despair. Man is free, — a god! man is bound, — a slave!

At one moment he believes he may accomplish whatever he may desire to do; and at the next moment he feels that he is little more than the serf of his environment. Wherever at any moment he may be, the wall which limits his wisdom rises ominously before him. He at one moment believes in his divine capacity, and at the next he doubts if he is anything but the dupe and plaything of cunning Fate. His longings and aspirations point him to the stars; he prays for wings to make his flight thither; he even begins to rise; and soon the chain is straightened, and he finds that his feet are held to the rocks and shoals of Time, — "Thus far shalt thou go and no farther."

II.

But it was ever the glad refrain of the ancient psalmist that when he had taken his flight into heaven, or descended down into sheol, he found himself not unattended. When the darkness gathered about him the

thickest, he felt most distinctly and impres-
sively the immanence of God. It was his
glory to have reached his own limitations,
and in every upward flight of wisdom into
a higher and broader outlook to feel those
limitations all the more keenly, because only
in those limitations could he realize the un-
limited and eternal. And so it has been with
all the inspirers of faith, — with Socrates,
Jesus, Paul, Goethe, Swedenborg, and thousands of others, — all feeling with Pascal, that
though the universe may rise up to crush us,
we are still greater than the thing which slays
us, because we know that we are dying.
Nothing but divine and eternal Life within
the soul can tell man that he is capable of
death. The daring affirmations of great men
draw the sting of the grave; for, being good
interpreters of God, they yield to all men
glimpses of that better life wherein our very
mental inconsistencies are turned to our
profit. What can be the secret of the great
faith of great souls? How are they enabled

to exclaim, without misgiving, that man is greater than the stars, more immortal than the everlasting hills, of more value than planets? It is good for us to put our trust in the confidences of the Christs, but may we never drink directly at the fountain whereat they are nourished? What is it which serves them as perfectly as demonstration?

Is it not this thought, namely, that we are individual expressions of God? Are we not units of the eternal Whole, forever coming into existence, forever unfolding, forever changing, progressing, struggling? And when we have expanded to wider ranges of sensibility to the spiritual forces playing about us, do we not cease to cling to the leading-strings of the great masters, and learn that we are hid with all the Christs of all time in God? Then, if we ascend up into heaven we also find Him there; and if we make our bed in the grave, behold, He is there! The sense of His presence foreruns our knowledge. Knowing Him to be near, we have " great boldness of speech." And the one thought which comes to us to raise us above the inexorable limitations of the flesh is this, — that though *we* see but a short distance, *He* sees all things. We then know that in Him we are made sharers of all true wisdom. He becomes the great Giver of the *personal revelation*, whispering, Thou canst not see, thou art of thyself blind and deaf and feeble even in thy greatest power; thou canst of thyself do nothing. But *I understand thee afar off. I remember that thou art dust. I know thy down-sitting and thine up-rising. I am acquainted with all thy ways. There is not a word in thy tongue, but lo, I knowest it altogether!*

III.

Thus God knows all that can be known about us. The Infinite includes the finite. He overshadows and permeates man. There is not a mother in all the world, tending her little babe, with feeble, pulsing lips, with fingers quivering in its sleep, with visions passing across its eyelids, with whispers of the wings of angels stirring its little dimples into life, — there is not a human mother in all the world hovering in love over her helpless, sleeping baby, who knows, or begins to know, a millionth part of what might be known of her dear child. And yet, with what knowledge there is on the one side and mere helplessness on the other, there is a power mighty enough to move the world between them, to see to it that nothing this side that mother's grave shall harm that child. But in the kindred thought of God, we have the same thing exalted to infinite significance! A weak, limited humanity on the one hand, a "Power more near my life than life itself" on the other. On the one hand a praying, struggling, hoping, courageous little personality, and on the other his infinite counterpart; and between them a power of union and sympathy which, if violated, would cause the moon to run blood and the sun to hide its face. How then can we fail to be confident? And why should we not exclaim from our housetops that " even the darkness hideth not from Thee, but the night shineth as the day !"

IV.

" Let us not live like foreigners in our own world." We have scarcely yet dreamed of the extent of our nature. For, allowing full consideration to our limitations, all things are ours, " Whether Paul, or Apollos, or the world, or life, or death, or things present, or things to come, all are yours ; and ye are Christ's ; and Christ is God's !" Nothing can be understood properly, no religion and no philosophy ; and, therefore, no mental, moral, or spiritual welfare is secure without first of all accepting God as the foundation principle. On that foundation rests all our peace in this life, our hope in the life to come. " In him we live and move and have our being." Honors of the world may tempt us, the inherent desire for power may lure us on, the longing for great achievement may become the passion of our lives; but after we have followed any course for a given time, the Eternal demands and, in one form or another, must have recognition. Then one cries, " Search me, O God, and know my heart: try me and know my thoughts . . . and lead me in the way everlasting, — " exclaiming thus because of all agencies that lead us there is one, and only one, that can lead us in the " way everlasting," and that one is God.

CHAPTER VIII.

MAN'S KNOWLEDGE OF GOD.

BUT if we do see that God is " all in all,"
and the life of all ; knowing us when
we know not Him, and caring for us as a
mother cares for her unconscious babe, how
may we recognize Him and be drawn to Him
until we become one with Him ? Upon this
possibility hangs the practical efficacy of all
religion. Can it be shown in the terms of
philosophy? Possibly. Can it be stated in
scientific phrases ? Possibly. But, best of
all, it may be taught in the symbols of human
experience. It may be worth our while to
notice that whenever anything appears in the
New Testament which could be construed as
a definition of God, the language is that of
experience, and not that of theology, philosophy, or science. How is it that Jesus ex-

claims that " I and my Father are one ?"
How is it that Paul writes of God as a " God
of patience and of comfort," a " God of love
and peace," and " one God and Father of all,
who is over all, and through all, and in all " ?
And how came the writer of 1 John to
say of him that " God is love " ?   It was the
simple language of experience transmitting
such wisdom as comes when man is brought
" face to face with the Eternal."   And as we
are now concerned with such wisdom, we have
no need to revert to any First Cause, any
Unknown or Unknowable, any Infinite and
Eternal Energy, from which all things pro-
ceed, any Power not ourselves making for
righteousness.   Apt and helpful as such defi-
nitions are to man's intellectual being, we
must pass them by that we may come more
closely to Him through the symbols of experience.   Can we not recognize God in the glow-
ing warmth of human intercourse ?   If you
have a beloved friend, you do not know him
by any estimation of faculty, any application

of square and compass, any test of scales.
Nor could you know him as a human soul,
were you to go to the extremity of the scalpel
and take down every particular portion of the
temple in which he dwells.   The scalpel is no
prophet, no seer, no revealer of spiritual
entities.   It is but the key which unlocks
the door of superficial knowledge.   And yet
you know your friend, even though you be
blind and deaf.   It is a knowledge which is
proved by its exceptions.   It is proved when
we exclaim in humiliation, "I did *not* know
him."   You had trusted him because you
thought you knew him; but your knowledge
proving false, you are in sorrow.   But where
it is not obscured by the sophistries of the
flesh, it is true, beautiful, and mighty.   It is
deeper than the books contain, higher than
systems impart.   It is the insight of the spirit.
It transcends the petty quibblings of man's
discursive faculty.   It is by this spiritual
knowledge that lofty friendships are made
possible, — friendships that can be relied upon
in every need of prosperity or adversity.

Such was the knowledge that the great teachers of religion have had of God. Men have always attempted to know Him intellectually alone, — one might say, physically. They have applied to Him only the standards of but one phase of their own small being, and have therefore failed; they have measured Him with their foot-rules, and called Him infinite; they have attempted to weigh Him in their balances of brass and gold, and have not succeeded; they have endeavored to dissect Him and to enumerate His " attributes," and have become bewildered. But any such conceptions as have thus been secured have not represented that Life which throbs in the universe, giving it its myriad forms of manifestation. At best they thus found but the vestiges of by-gone, lifeless deities of man's rudimentary past. In them is no glow and warmth, — nothing to fix one's faith upon, nothing to plant one's hope within. But when Jesus declared that " God is spirit, and they that worship Him must worship in spirit and truth," he revealed Him, not in the realm of discussion, but in the realm of life. The mother knows her babe no better after she has weighed it. The child knows not its parent according to the canons of physiology and anatomy and psychology. The truth is acquired by *spiritual association*. And when the physician has had his say, and the phrenologist has applied his test, and the grave specialist has made his examination, then the parent and the child, transcending the deliveries of the human intellect, lock each other in the embrace of spiritual sympathy, being made one through that Love which binds together all the constellations of humanity into the general whole which is God, — " God is love." And when it is said that " Thou shalt love the Lord thy God with all thy heart, and with all thy soul, and with all thy mind, and with all thy strength ; and thy neighbor as thyself," then is given to spiritual humanity what Newton gave to physical bodies, — the statement of a universal law of gravitation.   If, then, we are to recognize God and be drawn to Him until we are one with Him, it is in the same way that we are drawn to those who are dear to us, — by that spiritual association which is the inspirer of love.

CHAPTER IX.

MAN'S PRAYER TO GOD.

I.

AND what is the character of that association? I answer, it is the same as that which exists between human beings, and it is developed in the same way. To know each other we must be together. To be together we must so will. To know each other well, it sometimes requires years of voluntary association; it sometimes requires but a moment. We are to know God, and, knowing Him, to love Him in the same way. And if you ask, How is that association to be begun and continued? the answer is, By Prayer. Not by what men have been pleased to call prayer, but something more. Not by incantation, not by formal offerings, not by senseless begging; but by the retirement of the finite into the Infinite, the voluntary concentration of the human soul upon the inexhaustible Source of wisdom and strength. It is prayer after the manner of Jesus,— "Enter into thine inner chamber," and "This kind can come out by nothing save by prayer." The world has "entered in" from time immemorial; and yet much that has been called prayer is mere ritual, sometimes capable and often incapable of awakening the spirit to true prayer. The soul prays as the body breathes. Our lungs, when they feel the touch of air, heave and expand in natural response to the element which evolved them; and man's spirit, when it reaches consciousness, responds to the pressure about it of the divine Element of which it is the organ.

"When first thy eyes unveil, give thy soul leave
    To do the like; our bodies but forerun
The spirit's duty. True hearts spread and heave
    Unto their God, as flow'rs do to the sun.
        Give Him thy first thoughts, then; so shalt thou keep
        Him company all day, and in Him sleep."

True prayer, like true breathing, sustains life. Does the sleeping infant have any idea of what its breathing may accomplish? Let that breathing be intelligently cultivated, and it may speak on the tongue of a Cicero or a Chatham; it may soar in the song of a Patti; it may compel in the tones of a Bourdaloue; it may carry its possessor through the struggle or the race. So prayer is the normal effort of the soul to gain and increase spiritual life and strength. It is generally as fickle as the breathing of a sick babe; and yet, when we cease to pray, *we* cease. It expands our powers, leads us into invention and discovery and peace. Nor can it be said to be miraculous. It is as natural as any function. To regard prayer as the medium of the miraculous is the same as regarding breathing as a method, sufficient in itself, without the slightest voluntary training on our part, of singing a beautiful song. And as breathing is only a means whereby we may intelligently become sweet singers or powerful orators, so prayer is simply the means whereby we may perform good works and achieve great blessings. All true prayer, contrary to the view of many, is intensely practical. And just as there are two ways to breathe, so there are two ways to pray, — a right way and a wrong way. Let us suppose that one affirms that good singing is accomplished by good breathing, and that without good breathing there can be no good singing. It is true; but it is not the whole of the truth. One affirming this, and nothing further, might breathe hard and soft, explode his breath and suppress it, blow and puff; but if that were all, no song would come forth. Again and again he might try, and still no song! After many trials, he concludes that something more than breathing must be done. The fallacy is apparent. Of course no song could be sung without breath; but tone, and tune, and rhythm, and many other conditions must be observed to make the breathing effective. One might breathe

5

for eighty years, and never sing; and yet, not a single note can be executed without breathing.

We may say the like of prayer and praying. We may remark that " more things are wrought by prayer than this world dreams of," or even that nothing is wrought without prayer. And if one accepts this statement, with nothing more, he might utterly fail. Acting upon it, he might plead, and beg, and implore without moving Heaven by his importunity. And after long beseeching he might exclaim: " I have prayed long and ardently, because it is said that all things are possible to him that prayeth, and without prayer nothing can be wrought; and yet, my prayers are not answered." Is not the great error manifest?

Again, for the sake of convenience we say that the laws of music all exist; that all tones are possible, and the means are within our reach, and that we have the power by breathing of producing it. And here is the lacking condition. *We must apply all the laws of music to our breathing before the song issues.* And so with praying. The great inventor believes that there exist certain laws of sound which might be brought into such relations with an electric current as to produce the phonograph; and he enters into his "inner chamber" that he may discover those laws and bring about those relations. He feels sure that he is to meet there the Creator, both of the electric current and the laws that govern sound. He nothing doubts. It requires days, months, years perhaps, before the receptacle of his mind is sufficient for the revelation; but at last *his* importunity is rewarded. At first, by faint apprehension, he is made aware that a great fact is near at hand; then he sustains a sudden glimpse of a perfect law; then a perception of related forces; and so on, until his Sinai gives forth its secret. Beethoven, composing his Ninth Symphony in silence, beholding and hearing nothing that transpires about him, with a mind oblivious of all the distractions, the discords, and the troubles of his life, presents his petition to the Life of all. And at last the grand music breaks upon his mental ear. He hears it in his deafness, as if it came from the chorus of some upper world, and his whole soul is rapt in unutterable joy. Then he catches the spiritual sound, and places it where it may be interpreted into symbols of sense.

Thus prayer of the true sort, which is no mere jargon of meaningless words, makes all things possible. It moves mountains, builds dizzy towers and ponderous bridges, it girdles the globe with the human voice. In the Infinite Intelligence is a knowledge of all things. God knows how all things are accomplished. If man wishes to know, how shall he effect his purpose? Where shall he apply for knowledge and power? Why, where it is! We apply to Him. We turn our faces to Him, as the lily its petals, and we receive the thing our heart desires.

When our minds are receptive they are filled with bounties. In life's sterner experiences strength is given, in perplexity patience is given, and in our sorrow peace is given, by this pleading of the soul of man in his "inner chamber."

II.

This thought need hardly be brought into the more limited sphere of daily life. There is scarcely an hour which does not bring us before some obstacle which we must needs remove, some impediment which we must cast aside, some problem, great or small, which clamors for solution. And since in the empire of all wisdom and all love there are no insurmountable difficulties, we enter that spiritual empire for directions, and seek not in vain. What God wishes to have done on this planet through us, He can find a way to impart, if we listen. Surely, would He not satisfy all the longings of His children if He could find them attentive to the divine instruction? Our children are constantly asking us questions whose answers we would impart if we thought them capable of understanding us. We may know the answers, but they could not receive them, because the time is not yet. The spirit oftentimes expands in great pulses, and what we could not understand at all yesterday may be a platitude to-day. Be sure that when the Eternal finds within us a place large enough to write His revelations down, they will there appear as if written with a finger of light. And if we seek Him earnestly, His secrets will not be long withheld. Then the association between God and man shall more and more become like that which binds true friends together, and glimpses of the better life will assuredly appear.

CHAPTER X.

" AND the Lord spake unto Moses face to face, as a man speaketh unto his *friend.*" Abraham was also called "the *friend* of God." And this was so because the Will of the one was the Conscience of the other. If man's conscience be not God's will, then are we indeed as "clouds without water, carried along by winds; autumn trees without fruit, twice dead, plucked up by the roots; wild waves of the sea, foaming out of their own shame; wandering stars, for whom the blackness of darkness hath been reserved forever." In the realm of man's intellect and aspiration he seeks and finds companionship with God through prayer. But through conscience God seeks and finds companionship with man. Thus is the association of the divine and human reciprocal.

"I see in God both God and man;
    He, man and God in me.
I quench His thirst, and He, in turn,
    Helps my necessity."

Whether conscience be merely the result of the experiences of the race brought down through the generations, whereby we may choose that which will, in the long run, yield the greatest pleasure and the least pain, it matters not in our present considerations. It is a great fact, and a fact whose greatness cannot be diminished by the label we attach to it. Whether we frankly regard it as the voice of God warning us away from what is hurtful and urging us on to what contributes to our welfare ; or whether we reduce it to the cold formulas of science, it is yet that power which, in the region of our ethical existence, is as indomitable and terrible as the passion for the propagation of the species is in the sphere of physical life. Its genesis is far from being explained, but its presence in human affairs is an indubitable fact. We can trace with some degree of accuracy the devious line of experience; we can analyze, after a fashion, the course of knowledge; but whence comes this little candle that throws its beams into the hitherto dark world of the individual, no man can fully tell, except he receives it as coming from God. This sense which attends us on our way over the stony path from childhood to the place of peace, forever saying, Turn now to the right, now to the left; now pass thou up those dizzy heights, now down into those dreary depths and shades of night — what this may be in itself, and whence it came, if we knew, we should know the mind of the Eternal. In religion we delight to call it the spark of the eternal radiance shining into the soul of man, the voice of God speaking to man, or the principle of eternal life. It is so clear a light, so audible a voice, so noble a principle the world over, that we have come to trust it for much that we do not know and for much that in love and tears we hope for. It is the savior of the world from its own undoing. " It makes cowards of us all " whenever we are unfaithful to its mandates. And while it is the life-light to the righteous in whatever sea of trouble, it is a flame of hell to him who staggers in the jaws of infamy and crime. It prompts us to sing, as the lark, in the eye of the upper world; it wrings from us the cries of the damned in the lower regions of misery and vice. It is fearful and wonderful and in the style of God's mightiest works, because it is of him. In its sublimity we tremble, in its strength we glory, and in its promise we are at peace. It is therefore expedient for us to recognize it, on the divine side of life, in the same way that we recognize prayer on the human side of life, — as spiritual importunity; for conscience is the prayer of God to man. Prayer looks up unto the hills for strength, conscience looks down into the valleys for righteousness. Prayer is the cry of a soul

for help, conscience is the demand of Soul for
truth and virtue. They are the reciprocal
forces that hold humanity in the orbits of the
true life, and either without the other would
plunge the spiritual universe into confusion.

CHAPTER XI.

I.

IF, however, man is the " praying animal," he is no less the *anxious spirit*. And this anxiety has often led him into false views of life and fruitless pleadings for help. It has caused him to become impatient and even exasperated; so that, childlike, he has madly kicked and stormed at heaven's gate, as one beside himself. " Rest in the Lord and wait patiently for Him " he has not, and therefore has he suffered many times the consequences of his own indiscretion and folly. The very thought of prayer has thus become corrupted until it is turned against law and the divine will, instead of being made their ally. But great men have always shown their strength by their capacity not to hurry. The greatest

boon of religion is its assurance that whether
we labor, or whether we linger, if so be we
are true to our highest impulse, we shall reach
the goal of our noblest welfare. Is not that
the most delightful journey where we have
not to " make time," but may live large hours
of profitable idleness and drink deeply at the
fountains of " living water " ? Surely we may
say, —

" In some good time, his good time, I shall arrive."

When Jesus exclaimed, " Be not anxious
for the morrow," he knew that the anxiety
which corrupts prayer and all those sacred
relations which hold us to the Life of all, would
retard rather than advance spiritual growth.
Faithful men are confident of the integrity
of things. Anxiety is illness. The end of
spiritual endeavor is peace and confidence.
One would hardly think this were so were he
to cast a superficial glance over the pitiful
unrest of institutional religion. The seething and turbid competition of sects for the

mastery of the masses is no evidence of spiritual serenity, but rather an indication of
ecclesiastical vanity, which delights more
in temples made with hands than in the
houses eternal in the heavens. The zeal of
both Jesus and Paul was deep and earnest, —
deeper and more earnest than any anxiety, —
and it sought to uplift and save mankind.
But that was a very different thing from the
fever-heat which brings sleepless nights and
delirious days in the interests of organizations
whose main glory consists in long registers of
nominal converts and multitudinous forms of
real and personal estate. I do not deny that
in the terrible days when Cromwell and his
armies were laying waste the symbols of past
aspiration (those beautiful abbeys of Great
Britain, whose walls had for centuries contained the simplest and sweetest devotion and
quiet faith) they were largely resenting
wrongs and crushing abuses which violated
the decrees of a higher ethic ; but with it all
there flowed a spirit of unholy adventure and

greed which subsisted upon the exaggerated anxieties of the masses. And, further back, too, kindred abnormal expressions of this anxiety are everywhere found on the pages of history. When thousands abandoned the natural avenues of life and irrevocably committed themselves to ceaseless formalities, in protest, largely, against the excessive anxieties of a fevered state, we find innumerable evidences of a sin-sick and disheartened race. Paul the Simple, filled with the universal disquietude of his time, proposed to himself three hundred prayers a day, and was overwhelmed with distress upon hearing of a virgin who said seven hundred prayers in the same time. To " pray without ceasing " in that early age contained no thought of that prayerful peace of mind and heart which is the very essence of belief. Acts of piety were acts of distress and pain and mortification, and the exercise of every conceivable austerity, instead of the spontaneous utterance of human nature sheltered under the

wings of perfect love. Excesses of the spirit
then, as now, were manifested by excesses of
the flesh; and, in his anxiety, man believed it
his duty to flee from those " ways of pleasant-
ness" and " paths of peace " which render
our fickle and restless nature hopeful and
serene. It was as if men of a religious turn
were blind to those deep principles of the
spiritual life which were so familiar to the
founders of Christianity. They groped and
wandered in the wilderness, and, in their loneliness, called out through the darkness, —
called wildly, as children cry in rage or terror, — and would not be still that they might
hear the " still, small voice" of the Eternal
which whispered softly in their inmost souls.
In hunger and nakedness and sleeplessness
and self-inflicted torments certain salutary
lessons were learned, but only by setting at
nought many of the greatest achievements of
the old Hebrew and later Christian spiritual
life. They had learned to " hunger and thirst
after righteousness," but the time had not

come for them to be " filled," — to " rest in the Lord and wait patiently for Him."

II.

And yet " I know that whatsoever God doeth, it shall be forever." Life is life forever; and the Christ came that we might have that eternal life more abundantly. Where life is there is the superlative power. Nothing can essentially defeat it. It was the first promise looking to the creation of the universe, and it is still the end of universal hope. Life is never weary, never hurries, never fails " in His good time," to reach its appointed end. To gain it is the end of all pure religious effort; to broaden and cleanse the house for it to abide in is the true object of all education; to retain and increase and enjoy it is the boon of friendship between man and man, and man and God. Of the *living*, God is God. But life can never be defined. Its greatest and best witness is its own peaceful presence. It is the very climax of paradox

6

and contradiction when it is mentally considered. Men fear death, and then because of that fear kill themselves. "I ought not and cannot die," says one, "and yet I am dying." "Life ceases as we behold it, and yet it is immortal." All know what it is, and yet no one can tell you what it is. There is no intellectual demonstration of it; but in its activity and presence there is the indubitable proof of what it is. And after it has wrought upon these human bodies and awakened to individuality these points of divine aspiration and love, then it is manifested in its most beautiful phase, — that of surpassing peace and patient waiting. Such is the end of the struggle we are engaged in, the object of our prayers and the consummation of all philanthropy. No more feverish anxiety, no more travailings that cannot be uttered, but *confidence* and the *conviction* of *things not seen,* of endless welfare. Behold, the Prince of Peace shall come!

CHAPTER XII.

CONDITIONED as we are however, there are yet many things that we should know else we cannot arrive at the place of rest. We have beheld a glimpse of the better life, but the way thither is filled with hardships. If we have found God in our prayers, well! If through conscience He has spoken to us, well! If we have penetrated through the veil which our self-imposed anxiety throws over our spiritual vision, and have seen, in a single glimpse even, the promise of the " peace that passeth understanding," well! But we have not yet reached the second Eden; we have merely seen its reflection against the distant sky. We have yet to commend ourselves, " as ministers of God, in much patience, in afflictions, in necessities, in dis-

tresses, in stripes, in imprisonments, in tu-
mults, in labors, in watchings, in fastings,
in pureness, in knowledge, in long suffering,
in kindness, in the Holy Spirit, in love un-
feigned, in the word of truth, in the power of
God; by the armor of righteousness on the
right hand and on the left, by glory and dis-
honor, by evil report and good report; as
deceivers, and yet true; as unknown, and yet
well known; as dying, and behold, we live;
as chastened, and not killed; as sorrowful,
yet alway rejoicing; as poor, yet making
many rich; as having nothing, and yet pos-
sessing all things."

Surely, we are points of divine life, and
while we look into the eyes of our fellow-men
and behold the evidence of individual spirits,
we should not forget that they are rooted
with us in the Life of all. We have yet to
quicken our sympathies by large outlooks
upon mankind; to enliven our ideals by contact with the ideals of other souls; to break
up the troublesome incrustations that are

deposited by habit and routine, else we shrink below and behind the barriers of convention- ality, and become incapable of expansion. The sweet lesson of the Chambered Nau- tilus is ever with us, urging both mind and soul to build their "more stately mansions." In our present day when, as never before, the world begins to realize that "He Himself giveth to all life, and breath, and all things; and He hath made of one every nation of men for to dwell on all the face of the earth, having de- termined their appointed seasons, and the bounds of their habitation," ought we not also earnestly to proclaim the principles of universal brotherhood? The same great forces operate alike in all. In the simple child of the forest and in the strong repre- sentative of the Saxon race the same general spirit is at work expressing itself in the mani- fold forms of love and hope and aspiration. As time goes on and the nations of the earth increase their mutual interests, they must also more and more recognize their mutual obligations, until provincialism with all its petty conceits is no more, until the hatreds of parties and empires are done away, until war ceases and "the holy melodies of love arise." As water is purified by constant falling and evaporation, so human hearts must keep their currents fresh and strong by the perpetual intermingling of their sympathies. The cloister and the monastery may serve the world, but only after the world has given them food for assimilation. Solitude imparts eccentricity if long embraced. Harmony and uniformity of spiritual movements is more and more perfectly attained as the human spirit becomes sensitive to universal influences. In that heaven whose vestiges we have seen in the child-faces of the world and heard in the sweet voices of the true saints there are no provinces, adherence to no *patois*. Heaven is the "household of God" wherein we speak not of parties, cliques, sects, and nations, but of the "children of the living God." "None of us liveth to himself." The

thought of Rome and Ephesus and Thessa-
lonica must ever give strength, purpose, and
glory to Jerusalem and Antioch. Small
crotchets must be transcended, narrow pre-
judices must be outgrown, and in the life of
the world the individual must save his soul.

CHAPTER XIII.

DUTY.

I.

AND thus to press on over the wilderness to the light before, through trials many, we must have the sense of Duty. And that sense is more than expediency, more than the mere pursuit of pleasure, more than the warning of Fate; and it must be supported by all the agencies we have thus far dwelt upon, — by the sense of God, by the communion of the divine and the human through prayer and conscience, and by the presence of spiritual confidence and peace. The consideration of Duty may well be referred to the province of concrete experience.

II.

One is delayed at a distant and obscure railway-station in the heart of the Sierras.

While waiting wearily in the rude little building which serves as a shelter for freight and express boxes and packages, and for passengers as well, he suddenly hears the clicking of the telegraph. He is unable to read the message by the sound; but the operator instantly listens, and in a few moments leaves the room. Presently he returns and resumes his chair. What he has done, why he has done it, or what might be the consequence if he had not done it, the traveller is unable to say. In a little while the distant sound of an approaching train is heard, and mechanically the belated passenger looks through the little window and watches the long line of freight-cars as they come lumbering up the steep grade. At a certain point from the station the train stops. Then it begins to go through the mysterious evolutions peculiar to freight-trains, until it finally stands on a side track. There it remains motionless, the steam escaping regularly from the valves of the locomotive, and the trainmen standing carelessly about, chatting and laughing. Before long, however, the traveller's attention is arrested by the distant roar of another train. He again looks from the window, and at first beholds nothing. Then suddenly there comes in sight around the curve in the road a locomotive with great volumes of smoke and steam pouring into the air, with wild signals of whistle and bell; and scarcely has the looker-on time to note that it is a passenger-express before it flies by the station in the midst of dust and cloud, and disappears in the mountains with shriek and roar that awaken a thousand echoes for miles around. Then the traveller recalls the clicking of the telegraph, and he is now able to imagine the import of the message. It was the *duty* of the station-agent to receive, and having received, to heed it. It came from some far-distant manager of the road, and after passing through a long series of transmissions, according to a perfect system of railway regulations, reached its destination, — the

ear of that obscure agent in the heart of the
Sierras. That duty consisted in placing a
signal for the side-tracking of the freight-
train. Who could imagine the extent and
scope of the consequences related to that simple duty ? It was a very small matter for the
operator in that far-away place to hear and
understand and obey what was unintelligible
to the waiting traveller. But who could tell
what great issues hung upon his obedience ?
To say that upon it depended the happiness
of family groups in California, New England,
France, and Russia; to say that on it depended the business prosperity of houses in
Liverpool, Calcutta, Tokio, San Francisco, and
New York; to say that on it depended the
efficiency of colleges and universities, — not
to mention an almost interminable railroad
schedule affecting all the main lines of commerce and travel by land and sea, — is merely
to hint the importance of that single act.
That station-agent's duty was involved in a
vast scheme of human affairs. The message

came to him. He instantly obeyed it. It was to him pre-eminently "a still, small voice," and to him alone. Had he not obeyed it, the whole of civilization would have received a shock; for it was related to a vast labyrinth of well-defined elements of human happiness and prosperity, reaching to the farthest corners of the earth, and to the isles of the sea.

Thus we observe the character of Duty.

On a certain day and hour one sits quietly thinking. Perhaps the mists of every-day life — those half-clouds that prevent our seeing clearly into the higher strata of existence — have momentarily cleared away. Music, or an inspiring book, or a penetrating prophecy, may have put him into possession of himself. And he suddenly beholds a surprising duty. He is vexed that he sees it so clearly; he is not prepared for it; he would rather have known nothing of it. It is a duty that comes upon him boldly and irresistibly to give him disquietude. Others do not know of it, have not heard the message which came

to him alone, of all the world. If he chooses
he may disregard it. Mists of casuistry he
may invoke to obscure it. He may plead to
himself that he does not see what he knows
he does see; no one shall be the wiser. He
has it all his own way. God prays to him, but
he may fail to answer the petition. But the
station-agent in the heart of the Sierras heard
not more clearly the message of the telegraph.
If he persuades himself that he did not know
of the duty, or that it was the duty of another, he may enjoy a sickly self-justification
for his neglect. But in that case no one can
fathom the consequences. It will undoubtedly mean infinitely more either way than
the person interested can comprehend. The
message thus delivered comes filtering down
through the generations, finds its way through
the labyrinthine mazes of a complex environment, and reaches its destination only by a
power which is equal to the details of infinity.
Thousands, both now and hereafter, are related to it; and upon its observance their wel-

fare largely depends. One may heed it or disregard it, as he chooses,— the consequences he cannot compute.

III.

Nor is it for man to decide what duties are great and what small. The seemingly insignificant duties, owing to the conditions related to them, may prove to be vastly more deeply imbedded in the world's welfare than those which appear of greatest consequence to our limited vision. Nor does it suffice for those creatures of God who have a sense of duty to drift along through life as do those who have no such sense. The alligator lies basking in the sun, or floating on the water like a log, eating and sleeping, from the time of birth to the time of death. But that is the life of a reptile, and in living that sort of life it undoubtedly gives expression to all its faculties and powers. In human beings, however, there are many powers superadded to those of the reptile. The ability to think, to remember, to foretell; the ability to invent, and to venture beyond the limits of any known bounds of heredity, we find in the human creature. The "categorical imperative," or God's prayer to man, is forever his attendant. The human creature has the powers of both Gabriel and Lucifer. Both heaven and hell environ him, and he may listen to the voices of the angels of light, or to those of the angels of darkness. He does not know what the ultimate purpose of human life may be. He may feel very sure regarding certain things which cannot contribute to that end, and he may have great confidence in certain tendencies which he believes flow toward the highest and best. He knows that the great Purpose of life is not best realized through theft, lying, fighting, gambling, self-abuse, and murder; nor through incontinence, cruelty, negligence, and irreverence. He knows this because, while his sense of duty has told him plainly to be honest, magnanimous, and pure, he has absolutely no faculty, inherited or acquired, which admonishes him to be the reverse. And this sense of duty, which will not be put off, making itself felt sometimes forcibly, sometimes feebly, is the way the Eternal has of informing us what he wants done on earth; and we have every reason for concluding that the sum-total of these very small duties which are dictated to us as individuals, in the infinite variety of our conditions, will culminate in the accomplishment of His Purpose.

IV.

This is one of the obvious results of simple monotheism. "I am God, and there is none like me." But so long as men believed that there were others like him, so long the merely human sense of duty signified very little. A sense of duty to do this or that might then be interpreted as the will of one god, against whom another god might come and reverse the line of duty. An infinite Intelligence in Unity is an absolutely necessary hypothesis if we would have an adequate authority for righteousness. It is thus that we are ena-bled to believe that, so long as we heed His directions as they come to us from hour to hour, so long are we perfectly *safe*, and are bound to arrive, sooner or later, at the haven toward which the world is being piloted.

V.

And does one ask, How am I to recognize my duty? Listen! To him who listens *con-scientiously* the tongue of Duty is never dumb. If that voice be not stifled nor drowned in the babblings of selfishness, it must be heard. Too often does man turn away when the divine whisper is heard, and fool-ishly addresses some hapless spirit of Time. He easily holds out his hand to superficial Pride, who greets him with her conventional smile, and flatters him with her age-old com-pliments. He never thinks of asking *her* what his *duty* is. She does not wish him to consider real things. Her realm is that of

7

the unreal. She wishes him to consider what may be the easiest thing to do, or the pleasantest; how he may live with fewest responsibilities; how he may pass through life without any heavy burdens; how he may hoard (for who knows what?) the paltry gleanings of avarice; how he may find short cross-cuts into felicity, and by all sorts of intellectual jugglery avoid a meeting with Duty face to face. Duty is a divinity which will not sacrifice man's highest happiness to present pleasure. Other divinities will. They are short-sighted. They seek to make life pleasant now and to-day, without arousing a thought regarding the essential nature of human life. Such divinities, worshipped and grovelled before, will grant anything which Duty will not grant. And their slaves are legion. Why slaves? Because, while they at first furnish the superficial pleasures of time and sense, — enough to eat; a pleasant, narrow, selfish, childless home; opportunities to enjoy one's *self*, to be moral invalids far

into the age of manhood and womanhood, —
they allow it all that they may the better
fasten the manacles of a disgruntled, fruitless, painful, hopeless maturity and old age
upon their cringing victims. But Duty will
not do this. Duty will callous the hands,
painfully (through varied experience) expand
the mind, bind one to-day that he may be
released to-morrow; she will lead one
through dark and dubious passages now that
he may reach the light hereafter; she will
furnish tasks innumerable, troubles sore,
hardships and temptations many; she will
give him the cross that he may have where-
with to gain the crown. Slaves in this life
we shall be; but to be a slave to Duty in the
day of strength is to be a son of God, when
the slaves of shallow Egotism and Pride are
lingering in shame and weakness. Divine
duties are not always pleasant. He who
directly seeks the most comfortable thing,
and the easiest and pleasantest career, is
bound to reap dry leaves and the swine-husks

of mistaken hopes. The greatest of all human beings — the Messiahs of the world — have reaped eternal joy in the fields and vineyards of trial, where they have become men of sorrows and acquainted with grief, in the midst of burden-bearing and cross-carrying.

CHAPTER XIV.

THE KINGDOM COMING.

I.

MAN feels to-day — it has been a common sense now a score of years — what was felt at various periods in the history of Israel; what was, long before, felt in the Egyptian civilization; what seemed to be diffused throughout the empires of Montezuma at, and just before, the coming of Cortez into the New World. It is a sense of coming events, casting all too often their shadows rather than their lights before. There is, all true prophets declare, a new "Dispensation" near at hand. Its forerunners are already on the field of action. Already a cry from Russia, from one wellnigh dressed in camel's hair and with a leathern girdle about his loins, is sent forth into the world, — a cry so penetrating, so fierce, so regardless of earthly consequences to his own name and fame, so loyal to Duty, that men of thought stand amazed, cease for a moment their Pharisaic quibbling, and grow serious and thoughtful while his voice is heard. He draws his pictures of Church and State and Society and Business in a great, bold, Herculean hand, and in their essential features the portraiture comes so near the convictions of honest men, that only a feeble applause is elicited. Our times are as critical of danger as they are pregnant with vast promises and possibilities. The traveller in the Brunig Pass beholds deep gulfs and dark ravines, as well as snow-covered, sunlit heights. And when one notes carefully the age in which mankind is now moving, he beholds on the one hand groaning, hollow caverns of yawning self-destruction, and on the other the possible mountain-tops of light and love. The former are known by the absence of a knowledge of and a fatal disregard for the fundamental, as distinguished from the superficial needs of human nature; by an abandonment to a wrong theory of life and its proper objects; by a stubborn blindness to what we are on earth for, and a blindness, too, to the self-imposed slavery in which a large part of the world is submerged. The latter are known by the prophecies, here and there, of a better time; by the growing sense of mutual responsibility; by the careful attention given by honest men to the voice of Duty; and by the longing which many have to come down to a simple, truthful, childlike, faithful, and sympathetic plane of living, as distinguished from that of perturbation and strife, as now predominant. That better time must come by man's endeavor to answer the prayers of God; by man's attentive heed, without any thought as to what is easiest, or as to what is most commanding, or as to what is most pleasurable, to the voice of Duty as it is heard by the individual.

II.

Herein is the revelation of the New Life, — the Scriptures of the New Dispensation. They consist in the sum-total of the revelations of duty given to the individual souls of men. Does one ask how he is to recognize those Scriptures? Just as one recognizes the personal revelation from the Bible, from Homer, from Plutarch, from Shakspeare, — that in them which appeals to and is related to the personal experience. Not everything in the Testaments, not everything in history, is applicable to the needs of a given individual, but that part which fits into the vacant places of his life. So it is with the Scriptures of the New Dispensation. They are now being compiled, as were the Hebrew writings, by the flowing into them of myriads of human elements, wrung from the hearts of myriads who recognize God working in the affairs of men. Therefore, if one would know and profit by those scriptures, he must be attentive to the Voice which utters them, the voice of Duty, — God's prayer to Man. Such revelations, and such alone, are divinely inspired. Every individual duty is related to every other individual duty under the sun. And only that Power which is able to comprehend the infinite complexity of vital forces can dictate to individuals, as individuals, the special lines of true progress. That such lines are clearly indicated to men and women the world over, is evidence that the Revelations of Time are gradually being unfolded for the salvation of the world.

CHAPTER XV.

TRUTH : TRANSIENT AND PERMANENT.

I.

BUT is the earnest seeker after truth still puzzled as he recalls the errors and the false doctrines upon which generations have subsisted, thinking the while that they were living by "every word which proceedeth out of the mouth of God"? Does he cry painfully, that what may come to him as the very revelation of heaven, may also prove in time to be "as the morning cloud, and as the dew that passeth early away; as the chaff that is driven with the whirlwind out of the threshing-floor, and as the smoke out of the chimney"? This is a natural inquiry for one who beholds so much which is passing away, which was once adhered to as such vital truth that the stake and the rack and perpetual imprisonment were cheerfully endured rather than its surrender or denial. Especially is this true regarding many of the deliveries of Christian theology. Beliefs that our fathers thought should be embraced with all the devotion of the human heart, upon which the eternal welfare of the race was supposed to depend, have passed out of the practical creeds of to-day, and bear no relation to the methods of modern prosperity. If they are retained at all by thoughtful adherents of the Church, their original content has long since been displaced by new interpretations, or entirely reasoned away. They remind one of the ruins of feudal castles, once so famous, so fruitful of heroism and romance, so lofty on their perches above the troubled sea, so attractive to the novelist and poet; but now, in the light of modern engineering, so frail, shrunken, unwholesome, and even pitiable. The entire age within which they rose to the dignity and grandeur of a noble heraldry has passed away. And it is largely so with the central dogmas of mediæval theology which composed the intellectual feudalism of Christian history. How proudly has the Church and her sub-divisions stood in the royalty of Infallibility, referring to her Ecumenical Councils as to so many memorable tournaments where all the differences of human opinion were forever settled ! How earnestly they were fought out, with what tenacity were they defended, and with what heroism were they assaulted ! And now behold, mankind survives, and the very doctrines over which so much erudition, eloquence, and wrath were enlisted have, for the most part, become mere tiresome formu-las with scarcely a sign of their old-time vitality. They have vanished from the prac-tical concerns of the present day ; and beside the mighty revelations of modern science they are little else but crumbled ruins, — pictur-esque perhaps, but typical of a world which, beside that of to-day, is small, shrunken, and feeble beyond the telling. Nominally, they are still held by many Christian institutions,

but much as ancient ruins are preserved, —
because they are the symbols of the strifes,
the convictions, the trials and tears and mar-
tyrdoms of the past. They no longer awaken
the spirit of heroism, save in the breast of
some Don Quixote who so far forgets himself
as to mistake the century in which he lives.
They no longer breed a race of Crusaders,
nor that spirit which once sent strong men
to the dungeon.

II.

These considerations may well lead the
puzzled seeker after truth to ask if anything
wrought out of the human mind is abiding.
He exclaims that a like fate may await the
fondest conceptions of his own intellect. And
if so, why need he connect them with his
sense of duty, and project them into the
world with a plea for their reception? When
the next generation comes upon the scene,
will not all these religious beliefs, by which
we now set such store, be cast aside, super-

seded or transcended? And if this be so, wherefore seek after the thing we call Truth? Why not acknowledge at once that we are the dupes of intellectual delusions, and prepare as best we can to become extinct?

Only a moment's careful thought is required, however, to observe that not everything which is wrought out by the human mind coming in contact with the forces about it, passes away like the morning cloud. Many of the great truths which the world has held, at least intellectually, are not transient, but as fresh and glorious as the sunlight, rising periodically as the sun rises upon a waiting world, or shining perpetually in the consciousness of man to direct his steps in the paths of righteousness. They are the same in all times and places. No change of custom will ever subvert the Beatitudes; no revelation of science shall ever disturb the serene and princely supremacy of the two great commandments and the Golden Rule; no discovery and no invention can ever supersede or transcend the Fatherhood of God and the Brotherhood of man, — a doctrine which is not the creation of any Council, but the result of human experience, intelligible to every race. The Christian centuries have furnished us with innumerable practical truths just as abiding as these; and other centuries and nations not Christian have also contributed to the working wisdom of the world. The names of Aurelius, Cicero, Seneca, and Plutarch, and a host before and after, have left us storehouses of enduring thought which Time scarcely diminishes. And Thomas à Kempis and Luther and Melanchthon and Rousseau merely suggest an endless list of strong and faithful men whose influence in the interests of abiding truth does not wane. But no enduring monument is ever built without a superficial structure. There must always be the provisional scaffoldings, — they are absolutely necessary, but transient as the cloud. Many spikes must be driven where nothing is to remain. Great timbers must be raised, and thought and strength employed, only to be demolished within a brief time. And all this must be done in order that the true structure may be builded. The solid walls of the enduring edifice will remain, but the stagings — often imposing in themselves — must soon be removed.

Is it not so in history, in the realm of man's intellectual life? Sometimes it appears like a great waste of energy, this construction of innumerable local, provisional, and altogether superficial beliefs and opinions. And yet that which is permanent in human thought is made possible by what is transient. The transient is and has always been necessary to the recognition, not to say the production, of the permanent. We have but to recall the well-nigh interminable quibblings of the Jewish Gemara, to see that the great generalizations which Jesus finally submitted to mankind arose in the midst of a colossal accumulation of temporary intellectual results. The immortal spirit must have its

clay; so the great principles of religion and
the spiritual life must have their corruptible
husks. If our fathers had not mixed mortar
in beds that were soon to be thrown away; if
they had not spent many a monotonous century in constructing the crazy landings on
which the master workman could stand; and
if millions had not thought it honorable just
to carry the bricks and other small mate-
rials of the structure, this proud nineteenth
century could not have had its palaces of
learning and achievement.

Therefore the earnest seeker after truth
need not be disheartened by the consideration
that his minor beliefs may sometime pass out
of the working creeds of the world. It is impossible in one's own time to discriminate
fully what is to remain and what is to vanish.
But if each man is honest and also progressive, the question which concerns him most
will not be one of absolute truth, but a question of *need*. He must grasp the thing his
nature craves in order to have satisfaction.

8

It is the way of the Eternal to fill us with many desires, — to give us hunger that we may eat and live; to give us thirst that we may drink; to give us *ennui* that we may bestir ourselves to active interests; to give us passion that the race may be continued; to give us the longings that arise from grief and sickness and disappointment that we may have, and be able to extend to others, the anchor of hope and the balm of comfort. The aggregate of individual cravings ensures what is permanent. It is the duty of each to be true to himself, — to seek that which he needs. It may be only a provisional truth which will do him the greatest possible service now; but that provisional truth is for the time being absolute to him, and it will enable him to reach that which is universally absolute. "No chain is stronger than its weakest link;" so with one hour dropped out of life, life itself is broken; or one truth rejected, and the continuity of our intellectual progress is destroyed. If only man is true to himself at

any given time, honestly and earnestly appro-
priating that which his soul most eagerly
craves, he will be led into all knowledge and
all mystery, and fulfil the law of his being.
" Ask, and it shall be given you; seek, and
ye shall find; knock, and it shall be opened
unto you; for every one that asketh, receiv-
eth, and he that seeketh findeth, and to him
that knocketh it shall be opened." " Ye
shall know the truth, and the truth shall
make you free."

CHAPTER XVI.

MAN'S STEWARDSHIP.

A ND Truth, as we honestly hold it, is to
be *thrown* into the world. Men are set
as stewards over certain small demesnes of
life containing physical, mental, moral, and
spiritual capabilities, all controlled by the
self-same Spirit. It is for him to care for and
develop the estate, and cause it to yield fruit
for himself and the Lord of all. It is not for
him so much to calculate results as it is to
provide for them. Jesus described a sower
who went forth to sow. The seed fell here
and there, but the sower is not represented
as officiously watching where each kernel fell,
to see whether it would drop on the proper
kind of soil. It was his concern to sow liber-
ally of the seed. Some of it fell on the highway, some of it on the rocks, some of it

among thorns; and only a very small propor-
tion of it found the conditions where sun and
soil and moisture enabled it to yield its multi-
fold of grain. The sower is not portrayed as
one of the exceedingly careful people of the
world who are not disposed to do anything
unless they can anticipate to a certainty a
definite returning bounty. The great em-
phasis of the Parable of the Sower lies in its
teaching of abandonment to the immediate
task before him, and not in the anticipation
of the harvest. Spiritual rewards can never
be predicted with that exactness with which
the financier computes his dividends. For
the manipulation of "affairs" we have to
rely largely upon logical processes of thought;
but when we come to the realm of spiritual
force, our nice logical distinctions are very
apt to prove of slight value. The soul is not
dependent upon the syllogism. The forces
we deal with are so multitudinous, and the
results are of such a complex character, that
one becomes utterly bewildered who endeav-

ors to reckon beforehand the profits of well-doing. We are tempted to say in spiritual things, as in things material, that seed thrown upon shallow soil will amount to nothing, and so withhold our hand. Experience, however, teaches that man has no power to determine what soil is shallow and what is deep. The most astonishing wealth of spiritual life often arises where we had least expected it; and where we had looked for the most glorious manifestations of the divine, we are often equally astonished to find none. Truth, such as we honestly hold, is to be *thrown* into the world, wherever opportunity arises. God, in His prayers of Conscience and the sense of Duty, urges us to *do* with what we have. He reserves the right and the power of bringing forth the fruit of what is done by us. We may provide food and seek fresh air; but He attends to the assimilation of that food, and the operation of breathing. So it is for us to seek truth and cast it into the world; He will attend to its germination or to its dissolution, as He sees fit. It is by the acquisition and distribution of truth and aspiration that we are carried toward the second Eden. And, as by grasping with his wings and casting away the air in which he moves, the dove is borne to the uttermost parts of the earth, so it is by the rhythmical oscillation of our spiritual pinions that we are carried to the gate of heaven. "Whisper not to thy own heart," said Carlyle, "how worthy is this action; for then it is already become worthless. The good man is he who works continually in well-doing, — to whom well-doing is as his natural existence, awakening no astonishment, requiring no commentary, but there like a thing of course, and as if it could not but be so." This concentration of the human mind upon the thought of future rewards and punishments has often been a positive hindrance to the cultivation of spiritual powers. It implies that we are separated from and independent of the Life of all, and are therefore to be exactly compensated for the good

we do, and exactly punished for the evil we
commit. But no standard has ever been given
whereby human judgment is supported in its
decrees of good and evil. Our good may not
be so good as we think, and our evil may be
turned to more profit than our good. The
true steward is simply *faithful*. He labors
conscientiously, answers the prayers of his
Lord, and asks not, Wherefore those prayers?
It may be possible, for aught we know, for
the Eternal to teach his truths by means of
our errors; but it is the verdict of all noble
living that it is much easier for him to impart his truths by means of our integrity. It
is our business to be faithful to the Eternal;
to do his will as we understand it, and to
grasp such truth as we can comprehend and
transmit to other generations, and leave the
matter of reward to him. Melchisedek left no
annals, Homer no biography, Jesus no commentary, Shakspeare no personal reminiscence.
Their very greatness consisted in their freedom from *self*-assertion, and their absorption

in the work of life. They stood to transmit what came to them, to cast their seed, to *throw* it away. Surely "I of myself can do nothing; but the Father that worketh in me." As individual men they are scarcely more than myths and fictions; but as stewards they are the mightiest forces of civilization. And in what way did they furnish us glimpses of the better life?

CHAPTER XVII.

MOST of all, the world's great stewards have given us clear glimpses of the integrity of the universe. And they were able so to do because they themselves, standing near the Life of all, were made to assume (without question) the indestructibility of life. We read their thoughts, and those thoughts introduce us to what is grandest in ourselves. With skill they unlock the vast temples of belief and hope, of which we are the doors. At the hands of Isaiah we are admitted into realms of righteousness and peace; at the hands of Jesus we are ushered into the Father's house; at the hands of the master-dramatist we look upon the remorse, the vengeance, the burning love, the relentless shame, and cruel hate, and all the longings, hopes, and assurances of the human heart. And yet all these things were

in ourselves, unknown to us until revealed by
them. Few among men could stand at the
entrance of Life and reveal these things,
— only those who had a superlative *faith*.
They could look, like the eagle, upon what
would dazzle or fill with terror the ordinary
spectator; they could handle Despair as a
child would play with a toy; they could abide
with the sorrows and woes of our existence
and not be cast down; they could deal with
Love and Passion,— those forces that enchant,
that torture and consume, that twist and knot
our temples in indescribable suffering, — they
could present to the world their intensest
phases, and not lose their rapture in the glow
of life. They are of the few to whom both
heaven and hell opened, for they lead us into
the wildest storms that drive men to suicide;
into Gehennas of sin, misery, sensuality, and
death, and into the loftiest regions of spiritual aspiration and trust. And while they
place our fingers on the sinews of Death and
bid us lie down in the grave, by virtue of

their perfect freedom with these hideous
forms they prove to us that, beyond the
crimes that man enacts before his own conscience, these things have no substance and
no reality. Their confidence in the integrity
of the universe is so great that they could
mingle with life's greatest terrors without
being terrified, — as if it had never occurred
to them that in God's world there had ever
been occasion to be afraid.

It is therefore for one to build cities, for
another to train minds, for another to make
a home, for another to care for the poor and
wretched, — all to work with God, one no
greater than another in the Father's house,
all working with His voice to guide, all happy
in the one sufficient thought that " all things
work together for good to them that love
God." His forces play upon us, give us the
warmth of love, the gladness of light, the
freedom of hope, and the certainty of never
drifting beyond His power to draw us to
Himself.

CHAPTER XVIII.

I.

FAITH is the foundation of all belief. It is a necessity of thought. It is alike true of the Scientist and the Priest, the Theist and the Atheist, the Gnostic and the Agnostic. Some acknowledge and some deny its presence, but it is nevertheless the basis of all opinion, whether hidden or revealed. The physical scientist takes his refuge in observation, but he must have faith in the integrity of his powers of observation; or he bases his great doctrines upon the Atomic Theory, or the theory of a Luminiferous Ether, either of which is, in the last analysis, an intellectual absurdity. The agnostic paints his grand scenery of Life; but his canvas is the "Unknown and Unknowable" in which he places implicit

faith, as being a background which will always and everywhere receive his pigments.
The evolutionist assumes his First Cause, and
the materialist his Mind-Stuff, just as the
geometrician does his Axioms. "Faith is
the substance of things hoped for and the
conviction of things not seen." Wherever,
therefore, there is a "conviction of things not
seen" (and in the realm of man's intellectual
life we find it to be a universal condition)
there is *Faith.* Its ultimate object has many
names, according to that particular phase of
Truth upon which the believer gazes; but it is
always and everywhere the self-same Reality
which in spiritual language we call God.
Thus, an able student of Life has declared : —

"We cannot think far in any direction without
coming upon that which is more than all our
knowledge, — something that is and must be in
itself unknown, not because it is uncertain, but
because it is far too *real* for our superficial faculties. We cannot mark phenomena without thinking of substance. We cannot admire the ordered

system of the universe without aspiring in imagination to law above law, until at the topmost height one inconceivable stream of force springs into a myriad channels of harmonious action. We cannot feel the world's heart beat in the ceaseless energy of living things without adoring an all-pervading Life. Yet substance, law, power, and life are only names of the unutterable, — the last murmur upon the lip when different paths of knowledge open on those measureless contemplations which command the worship of silence." [1]

II.

"A mighty Hand, from an exhaustless Urn
Pours forth the never-ending Flood of Years."

The sense oppresses him of something against which man cannot prevail, so great its protecting care; of some Power in whose enduring grasp all lives are held; of stars obedient to an unseen Will; of an infinite flood of circumstance which sweeps all before it, — past the early days, the ravishments of his

[1] J. Allanson Picton in Mystery of Matter, pp. 127, 128.

first burning love; past homes on earth whose
inmates call out through the tumult of experience; past friends, children, parents, down
the quick years! Then he cries, —

> "O thou great movement of the Universe,
>   Or change, or Flight of Time — for ye are one!
>   That bearest silently this visible scene
>   Into night's shadow and the streaming rays
>   Of starlight, whither art thou bearing me?"

Then spiritual Faith arises to lead him to
the place of Rest.

CHAPTER XIX.

THE EDEN OF THE SOUL.

I.

THE place of Rest is the state of spiritual tranquillity. It is realized when we feel *at home* in God's world. It is where, under the inspiration of loving adoration, man brings every wayward, cruel, destructive, and vicious tendency into subjection to the will of God. On his way he encounters many temptations, many sorrows, many conflicts, much remorse and shame; he climbs and falls, climbs and falls again, in days of toil and nights of anguish, until the burden of every prayer and the essence of every desire is *rest*. The wise parent thus reads the future of his children, which is but the reflection of his own past, — toil is to dog their steps; the lack of bread

9

will cause them to stumble and faint and
fall.   Their faces, always the same in a
parent's eyes, will be stained with tears and
creased with suffering ; their hands will be
lifted up for help.   In the midst of their
later joys they will catch swift glimpses of a
more joyous past that they once knew, and
hope will be deferred and the heart made
sick.   This, he knows, is the common lot of
the generations.   Therefore, as long as human beings are here subject to hard work,
disease, and bereavement, they must seek, if
haply they may find, the place of rest, — of
spiritual tranquillity.   In a world which
stretches, as does this, between two Edens,
man must have the kingdom of God within
him, else he cannot know the blessing of
true peace.   So a prayer for rest becomes
universal.   It was the Nirvana of the Bud-
dhist, the goal toward which the prophets and
psalmists of the Old Testament set their gaze,
and the promise of the Son of Man.   "My
presence shall go with thee, and I will give

thee rest." "There the wicked cease from troubling; there the weary be at rest." "Oh, that I had the wings of a dove! Then would I fly away and be at rest." "Return unto thy rest, O my soul; for the Lord hath dealt bountifully with thee." These are but a few of the instances where the great spirits of Israel expressed the universal longing. And when Jesus cried, "Come unto me, all ye that labor and are heavy laden, and I will give you rest," he simply bespoke the last and pro-foundest prayer of the struggling and aspir-ing soul of man, after it has fought the good fight of the faith.

"Father, the shadows fall
    Along my way;
  'T is past the noon of day.
My ' westering sun ' tells that the eve is near
I know, but feel no fear.
And loved ones have gone home,
    A holy band :
I hear them call me from the spirit-land, —
    A gentle call.
Yes, dear ones, I shall come.

"Oh, not alone! though now
 I lead the van,
And with uncovered head
Press on where others led
 When my young life began.
I am not left alone,
Though they are gone:
Sweet voices of the past,
 And of to-day, —
The loved, that round my way
Still twine about my heart,
Tell me how good thou art.
 O holy Light and Love,
Beam on my soul,
My inmost life control:
Then may each pure thought spring;
And *peace*, with gentle wing,
 Brood like the dove."

II.

" There remaineth therefore a sabbath rest
for the people of God."   Not, to be sure, the
rest of inactivity and total passivity, as our
fathers may have dreamed; but the rest
which comes from that fulness of life which
knows no weariness, that culmination of trust
which allows no doubt.   Behold! the week

of toil is over! The spirit of man looks
forward to conditions of felicity which this
life was never intended to afford. Here is
the place of birth, the place of doubt, of pain,
of mental agony; it is the place where one
generation labors that another generation
may come forth, and the endless succession
of human beings be thus continued forever.
And what real happiness comes, what joy,
what gladness in the cup of life, is incidental
to the main issue and is the fruit of spiritual
transcendency over opposing forces! Incidental also to the rough conflict which man
wages against the elements of dissolution is
this glimpse of the " bliss beyond compare "
which he knows to be the natural dower of
the human soul. Forward then, the week of
toil being over, he sets his gaze. All is fresh
with the glad premonitions of the coming
daybreak, which is soon to steal over the
darkness of the life of sense. He casts away
all those vexatious cabals into which his intellect once plunged with resistless impetu-

osity. Questions which once absorbed all the
energies of his mind and gave to his mental
life that exhilaration which it once needed
for its devotion to duty, he now regards as
the toys and playthings of spiritual infancy.
His sorrows annoy him no longer, for they
have been his mysterious angels in disguise, —
entertained against his will, that he might
find the place of rest and be *at home with God.*
Passion is over, hate is done away, doubt
disappears, fear has fled ; the aches and pangs
of remorse have served their purpose, and are
no more. He has struggled for immediate
ends within his range of vision, but now sees
that he really labored for ends that lay beyond
the reach of his imagination. He was led by
a way that he knew not, but thought he knew.
And so he has proved his soul while he
imagined that he was only caring for his body.
All things have conspired to lead him ; the
child-faces, the sweet homes, the vistas of
youthful romance, memories brought forward
into after years, the admonitions of con-

science, the appeals of nature and of art, the
charms of music, the sense of responsibility,
the yearnings for knowledge, the disgust of
satiety, the anguish of grief, and the gleams
of hope,—all have conspired to lead him to
this "sabbath rest." 'And now, blessed assurance! he is no longer an outcast, no
longer a wanderer over the rough plain, no
longer a seeker after the light, for the Light
bursts upon the near horizon. In his fulness
of gratitude he cries, —

"I have nought to fear — the darkness is the shadow
    of Thy wing,
Beneath it I am almost sacred; here can come no evil
    thing.
Oh, I seem to stand trembling where foot of mortal
    ne'er hath been,
Wrapped in the radiance of Thy sinless land which eye
    hath never seen.
In a purer clime my being fills with rapture; waves of
    thought
Roll in upon my spirit; strains sublime break over me
    unsought."

Then swells the refrain "I am the resur-
rection and the life." I live! I live! The

life that is I is God! I am from the begin-
ning, and knew it not! I am unto the end,
and knew it not! "The desert blossoms as
the rose!" "The wilderness and the solitary
place are glad." The way I came is a way of
triumph. I came, I wrought the works of
Him that sent me, I go to my Father's house
of many mansions. No tomb so strong, no
stone so great, no wounds so deep, no Time
so long, but over all and through all and in
all I now see the Spirit of all,— God! And
God is Love.

THE END.